Dark
Detective

Written by J.A.C. West
Illustrated by Oliver Lake

Dark
Detective

Contents

Titles in Full Flight Fear & Fun

Space Plague

Bubble Attack

Circus Scam

Evil Brain Chips

Football Killers

Skyrunners

Spook Manor

Dark Detective

Valley of Wisdom

Maxi Beasts

Badger Publishing Limited
Oldmedow Road, Hardwick Industrial Estate,
King's Lynn PE30 4JJ
Telephone: 01438 791037

www.badgerlearning.co.uk

2 4 6 8 10 9 7 5 3

Dark Detective   ISBN 978 1 84691 121 7

First edition © 2007
This second edition © 2014

Text © J.A.C. West 2007
Complete work © Badger Publishing Limited 2007

Series Editor: Jonny Zucker
Publisher: David Jamieson
Commissioning Editor: Carrie Lewis
Editor: Paul Martin
Design: Fiona Grant
Illustration: Oliver Lake

1. A note about ____ demons

Scotland Yard is the address of London's police: it is known all over the world for cracking crime and solving mysteries. But it has a secret – a big, dark, nasty secret.

In a gloomy office you will find a man with a long, dark overcoat. If you ask his name, he'll smile like a skull and say: "I'm Detective Max Darke, Demon Division."

Level One Demons: Not very evil but sometimes leave litter and steal washing.

They also eat small children who should have known better than to go out after dark.

Level Two Demons: Less common but like to pick fights with men who have more muscles than brains. Then they eat their brains.

Level Three Demons: Aaaaaaaaaagh!

2. A really bad day_

Max Darke looked at his computer.

The emails all said the same. The
Brood had arrived in the city: Level
Three Demons – a nest of them.
He had to hunt them down – and fast.

Max stood up slowly. He collected his weapons.

The Brood were staying at The Ritz hotel. They liked rich victims – said they tasted better.

Level Three Demons don't just eat people – they suck out their souls and then steal the skin that's left.

A Level One Demon has red eyes and green skin. A Level Two Demon wears a hoodie or a baseball cap to hide its horns. But a skin-stealing, soul-sucking Level Three Demon – they look just like you and me.

Max sighed. It was 9 am – already it was a really bad day.

3. The best hotel in town

The Ritz was the best hotel in town. Only very rich people stayed there.

The doorman looked at Max's dirty coat. Level Two Demon blood is hard to wash out.

Max scanned the room. A group of American tourists were talking and laughing while they waited for taxis.

It was too loud, too noisy for Brood – they liked to work quietly.

Max scanned the room again.

Everything looked normal.

Suddenly Max saw a man drinking wine. The man had a forked tongue. Now he had to get the Brood into an empty room, so no-one would see what was going to happen. He had learned that blood and body parts upset people.

4. A rock and a _ _ _ _ _ _ hard place

Heads turned as Sophie walked through the door of The Ritz Hotel.

Men stared and smiled; women stared and looked cross.

Sophie was a beautiful woman with long, red hair. The curls hung down her slim neck. The long hair hid the horns on her head – Sophie was a Level Two Demon.

Sophie stared at the Brood businessmen.

> If you help me kill the Brood, I'll renew your Demon Passport and I promise not to arrest you.

> Max, darling, you called and I came.

Max's skin crawled at the touch of her demon flesh.

5. Double trouble_._

It was easy. The Brood took one look at Sophie's beautiful hair and lovely smile and followed her to a private room.

Max watched as two waiters carried in ten bottles of wine. This was going to be expensive!

When Max entered the room, he saw Sophie standing next to a Brood who was dressed in the skin of a businessman. The skin looked a bit worn – human skin only lasted two or three days when a Brood wore it.

Max sprayed Holy Water. The Brood's
stolen skin started to fizz and bubble as
it burned the evil inside. It screamed.

Panic broke out. Brood were running everywhere. Sophie was firing Holy Water from a water pistol and laughing like crazy.

The smell of burning Brood filled the room.

One huge Brood ran straight at Max. Claws sprang from its hands and the human skin fell to the floor. The demon's orange eyes burned with hatred.

The claws dug into Max's arm and he dropped the Holy Water.

The demon opened its mouth, ready to take Max's soul.

Max tore the silver knife from his pocket and stuck it into the demon's leg.

Suddenly, Sophie saw that Max had used all his weapons. She had a change of plan…

6. Fangs a lot

His Holy Water pistol was empty.
It wasn't looking good. In fact it was
looking really, really bad.

Sophie advanced, claws and fangs outstretched. She was about to tear him apart, one arm at a time.

His hand brushed against his coat as he backed away from her.

He pulled the garlic from his pocket and started to chew quickly.

Sophie stopped in her tracks.

Max!
You wouldn't! I kept my part of the truce – sort of!

Then he breathed garlicky breath in her face.

Max watched sadly as Sophie melted into a pool of green goo on the carpet.

There was a knock on the door. It was the hotel waiter. He stared at the room: broken chairs and tables, burns all over the carpet and something green and sticky on his shoes.

Sorry about that. Send the cleaning bill to Scotland Yard police.

Max Darke, Demon Division, left The Ritz and went back to his gloomy office.

Tomorrow was just another day... for fighting demons.